The Book
of the
Sea

Desdemona McCannon

BLOOMSBURY
CHILDREN'S
BOOKS

For my family – D.Mc.

First published in Great Britain in 1999 by Bloomsbury Publishing Plc
38 Soho Square, London W1V 5DF

Text and illustrations copyright © Desdemona McCannon 1999
The moral right of the author has been asserted.

A CIP catalogue record for this book is available from the British Library.
ISBN 0 7475 3923 5

Designed by Dawn Apperley
Printed and bound by Tien Wah Press, Singapore.

1 3 5 7 9 10 8 6 4 2

INTRODUCTION

The power and the mystery of the sea have fascinated every culture around the world since the beginning of time. In this magical collection of stories, many big ideas and explanations of the sea's power and mystery are explored. Story-tellers around the world have looked at the vastness and abundance of the sea and wondered how it was created. They have wondered about the inhabitants of the sea and imagined a different world on the seabed, with wonderful creatures living in the uncharted depths. They have marvelled at the enigma of the tides and looked for explanations. They have wondered about the creation of the sea and earth and recast these events as myths.

In these stories the sea is shown to have many different faces. For some story-tellers it is a source of endless opportunities and of great enchantment. For others its power is overwhelming and represents a great challenge to all who travel on it. For others still, its vastness and mystery pose great questions. It is strong, and frightening, benign and cruel, creative and restorative, masterful and comforting. One thing is for sure, while all cultures share a fascination with the sea, they do not all come to the same conclusions about its benefits.

In this lovely book, the many different stories, with their various interpretations of the sea, serve to remind us that three-quarters of the earth's surface is still a vast romantic mystery for us all to enjoy.

CONTENTS

Rose Petal and the House Under the Sea

Caribbean Sea

Rose Petal's mother had died when she was very small. When her father got married again his new wife was cross and unpleasant, and brought with her her own daughter, who was older than Rose Petal. The stepmother made Rose Petal sweep the house and tend to the pigs, and never made her own daughter, who was called Granita, lift a finger. Rose Petal tried to be cheerful although she often cried herself to sleep.

One day as she was returning from feeding the pigs, her empty bucket fell and rolled over the cliff edge.

Bump bump bump it went, down the cliff-face. What was she to do? Her stepmother would be very angry when she found out.

Sure enough the wicked woman said to Rose Petal 'Well! You just going to have to climb down after it. And don't think about coming home until you got it again.'

So Rose Petal went back to the place that she had dropped her bucket and slid and scrambled down the cliff until she reached the beach. Unlucky for her the tide had come, and she saw her bucket bobbing away on the waves. So she ran into the sea, ready to swim out to get the bucket back when suddenly the ground vanished below her feet and she was falling and falling. She saw shoals of multicoloured fish, who watched her curiously then darted into gulleys and caves to hide. As

she came to the bottom, she could see a beautiful new land in front of her, with green fields and beautiful flowers and fish calmly roosting in the trees instead of birds.

Rose Petal was amazed and surprised by this magical land and looking around she saw a path which she followed until she arrived at a cottage where a white-haired lady answered the door. Rose Petal explained to the old lady what had happened – how she had fallen down through the sea and how she was lost and frightened and the old woman asked her into her little house. She said that Rose Petal could stay with her as long as she wanted so long as she helped her with the housework. Rose Petal happily agreed.

This was unusual housework though. For instance when she made the great white bed she was told to shake the pillows out of the window. Bright coloured pieces flew out of the pillows and shimmered up through the water. The old woman explained it was joy and happiness she was letting free into the world. She explained to Rose Petal that when she scrubbed the pans she was making people healthy, and when she made the bread it meant there was plenty of food in the

world. She showed Rose Petal another room with mirrors all round the walls. It showed all the people of the world running and skipping with gladness from the good work she had done. Rose Petal looked for her father but could not see him in the happy people.

Rose Petal lived there for a while, but she missed her father very much and soon she was so homesick and sad she knew she had to leave. One morning after her chores she asked the old lady if she could go home.

The old woman sadly agreed to show Rose Petal the path out, and said, 'When you reach the end of the path you will see two gates, one of gold, one of wood, if you choose the wooden gate you will get a good reward, but the choice is yours.' And the old woman filled up Rose Petal's bucket with good things to eat for the journey, because she loved cheerful Rose Petal, and was sorry to see her go.

Rose Petal walked for a long time and eventually came to the two gates. The golden gate glittered with many jewels and seemed to promise beautiful things ahead. The old wooden gate did not look so inviting. But heedful of the old woman's words she opened the wooden gate and passed through it. Rays of golden light fell on her face and as she walked the light touched her clothes and hair and face, and she became even more beautiful. All the food in her bucket transformed into gold and jewels.

She reached her father's house before dark and ran up to him laughing. He was overjoyed to see her and hugged her close, as he had believed she was drowned. He looked at her in awe as she was now so dignified and beautiful. The stepmother pretended to be pleased to see Rose Petal again, but inside she was seething with rage. Now her own daughter seemed even more ugly and mawkish.

Rose Petal told them the story of her adventure, how she had fallen through the sea to a land where fish lived in the trees, and she told them about the kind old woman.

'Why should you be the only one to be so fortunate?' said the stepmother. And she sent her grumpy daughter with two buckets to the cliff-face. 'And don't you think about coming back without them full of pearls!' she scolded.

The girl bad temperedly threw the buckets into the sea and climbed down the cliff, grumbling all the time, 'I don't want to do this! Rose Petal should go for me.'

But she was afraid of her mother, so gingerly she walked into the sea, and sure enough the ground disappeared and she fell to the strange world at the bottom.

Granita looked around her and found the path that Rose Petal had told them all about. She hurried along until she found the little cottage and urgently knocked on the door. When the door was opened she handed the two buckets to the old woman. 'Here. I have come to fill these with pearls. Hurry up,' Granita barked.

The old woman was shocked at Granita's rudeness and said 'You must help me with my housework first!'

So grumpily and ill temperedly Granita looked after the house. But the floor was not swept properly, the fire became choked with ash, the food in the cupboards went mouldy and grey. Granita pulled at the white pillows with dirty fingers, and did not bother to shake them out of the window.

Soon the Old woman looked in the mirror room and saw that Granita's housework had caused disease and unhappiness through the world. She called for the girl, who came in slowly and did not smile or look at the old woman.

'It is time for you to go back to your mother,' the woman said. 'I have given you some food for your journey.'

When Granita saw the buckets full of food she yelled, 'Where are the pearls like you gave to my sister? This ain't no way to pay me for all the work I done here!'

But none the less she grabbed the buckets and marched out slamming the door behind her. She began walking up the path to the two gates Rose Petal had mentioned. As she hurried along Granita muttered to herself, 'I won't choose the wooden one – surely much greater riches must come from going through the golden gate.'

The old woman was not sorry to see her go, and she now had to undo all the bad work Granita had made.

Granita arrived at last at the two gates. 'Look at the jewels!' she said looking up at the fine golden gates.

But when she walked through these gates, instead of treasure and pearls there was just a horrible smell. She looked down in disgust at her feet which were ankle deep in slime and when she looked in her buckets she could see it was not jewels and pearls she had been given! She staggered home, but nobody wanted to touch her when she arrived. Her clothes were covered in snails and her buckets were full of evil smelling mud. The worst thing? The smell never went away from poor Granita, however hard her mother tried to disguise it with sweetest scents and perfumes.

JACK AND THE MERROW

IRISH SEA

Jack O'Mara was a fisherman living in a tiny village down the coast from Galway. It was the sort of village that has only one street, with a church at one end, and a shop that is also a bar at the other. He had lived there all his life, as had his father and grandfather before him. He had always wanted to be a fisherman, and had learned from an early age about boats and seacraft. He knew where the fish were and how to mend and untangle the nets ready for the next day's catch.

At night while sitting around the fire unravelling the course netting, Jack would listen to his grandfather's stories. Jack's favourite story as a child had been the friendship his grandfather claimed with an Irish merrow that lived just a little further down the coast. 'Irish merrows are like mermaids, but not so beautiful,' his grandfather explained. 'They have green hair, their tails are stubby and covered with barnacles, and their noses look like a pig's snout. If you ever see one,

chances are he'll be wearing his red cap, which is called a cowrie. This is what lets him come to the surface, and if he gives you one to wear, you can visit his home on the seabed. My merrow friend had a weakness for puccine. Now puccine is a terrible drink, it can knock you down after two glasses. Many's the night with the merrow that I had to tip mine into the fire bucket so as not to succumb to sleepiness. For the danger is that the merrow can take your soul as you dream, and then you can never come back to the surface again.'

As the years passed, Jack was allowed to go out in the boat with his father and grandfather, but he never saw a merrow, although he was looking all the time. The tide washed ten years away, then fifteen, and Jack was fishing on his own. His grandfather died and was buried. His father was lost at sea five years later. Jack was sad for a while, but he lived with his sister in their family home, and the routine of bringing home the catch for her to cook each day helped him forget.

One day he was out in his little boat and a lack of good fishing had chanced him into unfamiliar waters. The day was drawing in, and the sky looked heavy, like

it was holding a lot of water. Jack was beginning to think of turning back when, through the gloom, his eye caught sight of a green glimmer. It was coming very fast through the water. It wasn't a fish that he knew, but whatever it was, it was a big one that was for sure.

'O'Mara!' He heard his name. Where was it coming from? Before he could make up his mind a pair of large hands were on the gunwale of his boat. A face soon followed, and he found himself peering back at the green hair and piggy snout of a real live merrow. 'O'Mara!' the merrow said. 'It is you at last, I was wondering when I would see your face again!'

'Ah,' said Jack. 'Its not who you think. My grand-father has been dead these fifteen years, and it is his grandson who you are speaking to. Good evening, sir. I've heard a lot about you.'

'Then come in out of the weather for goodness sake, and lets get acquainted with a bottle or two,' said the merrow, and handed him a red cap to wear for the journey down to the seabed. In an instant the two were

sitting by a cosy seaweed fire in the strangest parlour Jack had ever seen.

There were hundreds of seashells on the walls, and ship's caskets stood for chairs and tables. The figure-head of a great ship loomed over them like a bossy barmaid, and from the ceiling rows and rows of lobster cages flickered a gentle light over the walls of the cave.

They sat and drank puccine. The merrow said they had a lot of catching up to do. He told him stories of his grandfather and the visits he had made to this very room. Jack listened and drank, and drank and listened, and soon the room was reeling with words and lobster cages. 'Tell me …' he managed to say, 'what is that light coming from the cages?'

'Ah …' the merrow tapped his snout knowingly, 'those are the souls of drowned sailors. I swim up behind them as they fall, and the soul slips easily into the cage. Before they know it they are down here with me, instead of being up there with you-know-who!' The merrow laughed loudly at his joke. He left Jack looking up at the cages as he went in search of another bottle. Jack could see the name tags that the merrow had carefully laid across the lids of each one. It was a roll-call of the crews from every ship that had visited the Irish coast and fallen before it could leave.

He was feeling sleepy, and began to slump in his chair. But a chill thought made him sit up, suddenly sober. He remembered what his grandfather had said about falling asleep with the merrow. He did not want to end up in one of the soul cages. He got up and began to look along the lobster pots. He had had an idea.

Sure enough there was his own name, with the little flickering light wanly waving at him. Jack realised that his father had met this merrow too, those years ago. He had visited the room he was standing in now. But his father had fallen asleep and so his soul had been taken as he dreamed.

Jack could hear the merrow coming back, cheerfully announcing that a keg of puccine had fallen from a trawler not three weeks ago, and that

there was still enough for a few drinks yet. Jack quickly opened the lobster pot with his father's soul inside. Just in time he wrapped the light in his handkerchief, and put it into his pocket as the merrow came back into the parlour.

'Ah, there you are!' called the merrow, and seeing Jack standing up he looked at him suspiciously for a moment and then said, 'What, going so soon? If you must you must. But come again soon, you hear. Just put on the red cap, and I'll find you and bring you down. Now, off you go …' and Jack was off through the sea like a shoot of water from a whale.

Hauling himself into his boat, he checked his pocket for his handkerchief. It was still there. He pulled it out of his pocket and started to untie it. There was a bulkiness to it that had not been there before, and a slight squeaking sound. As soon as the fabric was unknotted a little sea swallow flew out and spiralled up into the sky above the boat. It swooped down and skimmed the water, which glittered in the early morning light, then off it flew into the sunlight.

Jack went home and told his sister what had happened. She said to him, 'Are you sure you haven't had too much puccine yourself?' Just then a bird flew through the open window and perched on the back of their father's old chair. It was the little sea swallow. 'Now will you believe me?' said Jack, as it began to peck crumbs from the tablecloth.

THE SEA COW

BALTIC SEA

There once was an honest fisherman and his wife who lived on a rocky island, just off the coast of Finland. Their living was hard and they were frugal in their habits, but they were happy. Each morning the fisherman clambered down the steep rock face to where his little wooden boat awaited. He spent the entire day fishing, and each evening he made the same journey in reverse to share what he had caught with his wife.

They hardly ever saw people from the mainland. However, one day a group of students arrived at the island in a hired boat. They were looking for rare sea birds. The fisherman introduced his wife to them, and the two offered what hospitality they could. As they all sat eating a meal of salt herring and sourdough bread one of the students asked the fisherman's wife if he could have a glass of milk. She was deeply ashamed to admit that they had no cow.

'Oh well then,' laughed the student, 'no matter, a glass of water will do.'

But long after the students had left, the fisherman's wife could not get the incident out of her mind. Every day she talked about getting a cow. She became dissatisfied and complained that their food was always the same. She wished that they could have cheese and butter on their bread instead of just fish paste.

The fisherman was surprised, and said to her 'What should we care if we have no cow? We have enough to eat, a roof over our heads and each other.'

But she lay awake at night consumed by the desire to own a cow. She thought and thought of a way to achieve this. Then she remembered a spell that her mother had sung to her as a child. It was supposed to charm the sea king into giving you your heart's desire and it went like this:

King of the waters, Ahti is your name
In the deep dark indigo sea
Fishes and pearls belong to thee ...

The song went round and round inside her head until she felt she would burst if she did not sing it. She quietly got out of bed. Still in her nightdress she put on a pair of gumboots and an old macintosh. Then she crept out of the little stone hut, clambered down the cliff face and got into the little wooden boat.

She rowed out to where she could see a patch of moonlight dancing on the water. When she was in its pale blue light she began to sing:

King of the waters, Ahti is your name
In the deep dark indigo sea
Fishes and pearls belong to thee
A thousand sea cows silver green
I ask you to give one to me.

As she sang, she rowed the little boat round in a circle, following the line of foam she had created with the oar.

After a while she stopped, and in the quiet and the dark she felt a little foolish to be out in the middle of the night in her nightdress and gumboots, singing a song she had not heard since she was a child. The night was calm, and the sea was silent, and nothing betrayed whether her charm had been heard by the sea king. She returned to the hut and got back into bed, lying wakefully until the morning light.

The next morning the fisherman rose early as usual and made his way to the little wooden boat. When he arrived at the cliff he was astonished to find a beautiful cow on the rocks at the sea's edge, calmly grazing on the dark green seaweed that grew there. The fisherman ran back to the house and calling to his wife said 'Quickly! Come and see this incredible sight!'

But his wife was less astonished, and she masked her triumph with her obvious delight. They enjoyed milk in their tea for the first time, and made delicious butter and cheese which they ate every day with their salt herrings and sourdough bread. The sea cow seemed to need no looking after, and went on placidly eating the seaweed at the shore's edge.

The fisherman's wife, drunk with the success of her venture, grew greedy and could not rest until she had charmed another cow, and another, and another,

27

and yet another out of the sea. They now had a herd, a fine one, which produced delicious creamy milk. There was too much for just the fisherman and his wife, and so they took some to the market on the mainland. Soon their milk was in demand. They were selling as much as they could produce of the milk and butter from the beautiful sea cows.

As the fame of the cows spread, the fisherman and his wife became comfortably well off, and then wealthy. The fisherman no longer picked his way down the steep rock face to his little wooden boat. Instead he watched as the wooden boxes of cheese and butter were lowered down by a crane to the waiting tugs below. Then he returned to his brand new house, its many rooms kept immaculately clean by a maid, and his wife in her finery, surveying it all.

All too soon the trappings of wealth changed his wife from the careful, patient woman he used to know and love into a harsh and greedy woman, quick to anger and too proud to forgive. She cared only for money and little for the fisherman and the island. She talked of taking the cows to the mainland and setting up somewhere with better pasture and easier routes in to the town.

She spoke crossly to the fisherman as they sat over a fine meal, and said to him, 'Without me you would have none of this! I have created all this wealth through cleverness, something you would not recognise if it

28

slapped you in the face.' And she tapped his nose with her fork to accentuate her point.

The fisherman walked sadly to the headland and looked out to sea. He could see the flotilla of little tug boats taking the cargo to the mainland, and below him were the sea cows grazing side by side on the seaweed covered rocks by the shore. He felt so unhappy he could have jumped off the cliff. The sea cows' greenish hides seemed to shimmer before his eyes. They began to look sinister to him.

Deeply troubled, he went back to the house and said to his wife, 'By whatever means you have got these cows, please let them be taken away again. They are the reason we are unhappy and I fear some great mischief has been done.'

His wife looked at him with a hard look in her eyes, and then suddenly burst into tears. The truth was she was not enjoying her life as a grand lady. She felt lonely, and was worried that her maid was laughing at her behind her back.

That night she rowed out to sea once more. Reaching the patch of moonlight and swinging the boat into a circle she sang:

> *King Ahti, hear my song once more*
> *My tears fall into the salt sea*
> *Each one a pearl to give to thee*
> *A thousand sea cows silver green*
> *They must be taken away from me.*

The next morning the cows were gone, and the fisherman and his wife woke up in their old hut, with just a string of herrings and a broken old chair.

29

SADKO

CASPIAN SEA

Sadko was a poor musician who lived in the town of Novrogod, by the shores of lake Ilmen. He had hair the colour of corn, and eyes the colour of the sea. Because he was poor the girls in the town would not smile at him. Instead he spent the evenings walking along the banks of the pretty river Volga, the river that ran into the lake. He thought this river was more beautiful than any Sasha or Natasha. As he walked he composed songs on his dulcimer to sing her praises.

To earn a few copecks he would guard the fishermens' nets as they went into Novrogod to sell their catch. One such night he was sitting on a rock, picking out a melody on his harp, and idly watching the moon rise over the lake. The ripples

of little waves running into the shore lapped the ground in time to his music. Then all at once they began to change direction and swarmed around the centre of the lake. A whirlpool was forming. Out of the hollow centre emerged a gigantic man, with a golden crown and blue hair flowing down his shoulders to his waist.

It was the Tsar of the Sea, and with a voice like the sighing of the sea he said, 'Sadko, you have pleased us with your music. My daughters love to hear you sing, and I too have listened with pleasure. Throw your nets in to the water and you will find something from us. If you accept this gift, you must come and play to us in the green palace of the sea.'

As Sadko watched, amazed, the Tsar descended into the whirlpool again. Soon the lake was as calm as before. 'There is surely no harm in throwing out a net,' he said to himself. So that is exactly what he did. Then, in the cold moonlit air he sang the song that he loved the best – in praise of the Volga, his favourite river.

When he pulled the nets in he discovered a small casket caught in the dripping ropes. Inside he found hundreds of precious stones, of many colours, which glittered and shone in the black air.

Sadko sold the stones one at a time, using them to buy at first a market stall, then a warehouse, then a ship, then a fleet of ships. He became a rich and powerful merchant and travelled all over the world in search of precious goods to bring back and sell in Novrogod. In time he forgot his promise to the Tsar of the Sea that he would play for him, but he did not forget the river Volga. Each time he returned from a trip he would take a small gift to the river and throw it in as a token of his regard.

All the girls smiled at Sadko now. 'Look at his blue eyes, the colour of the sea,' they said to each other.

Sadko continued as before. He could not find anyone as fascinating to him as the Volga river.

Twelve years had now passed since Sadko's meeting with the Tsar of the Sea and he was on a journey to trade with countries on the other side of the Caspian Sea. He sat on the deck of the ship and watched the stern furrowing the crisp water. The billowing white canvas of the sails sang in the wind and the ship was skimming across the surface. A song bubbled in his breast, and he took up his dulcimer and sang of Novrogod and the river he loved.

Then something very strange happened. The ship stopped in its tracks. It was as though a huge hand had caught hold of the belly of the ship. There was no land for miles around. The captain sounded the depths all around the ship and found that it was seventy leagues deep. There was no explanation. The sailors offered their own, 'There's a mischief in this!' they said to each other. The sailors were extremely superstitious, and they believed that someone on the ship was unlucky.

'When he is found,' they said, 'He should be thrown overboard.'

They drew lots to find out who was the cause. Sadko drew the short straw. He said, 'I remember now a promise I made twelve years ago. I have a debt that I must repay.'

He bid his crew a civil farewell and stepped from the ship. As soon as his feet touched the water the ship began to move. The waters closed around Sadko's head, and he began to sink to the bottom of the sea. As he fell he thought it strange that he was not drowning, and felt no need to breathe.

On the sea bed he saw a magnificent palace made entirely from the timbers of wrecked ships. The wood was green with age and algae. The gates were guarded by two huge fish. Sadko walked through the gate and saw the Tsar resting on his side in a Great Hall. 'Ah Sadko,' he said, 'at last you come to play for us. It has been a long time.'

Sadko began to play on his dulcimer and sang the sweetest song he knew. He sang of Novrogod and the beautiful little river so dear to his heart. The Tsar stood up. 'I must dance,' he said.

He glided out of the hall and through the gates where the two fish stood guard. The Tsar grew and

grew – he became twice his size. He was truly huge, and his feet pounded the floor of the ocean as he danced to Sadko's songs.

The sea's surface boiled and frothed, and ships were wrecked in countless numbers. Eventually the Tsar stopped and re-entered the gates, shrinking to enter the Great Hall once more.

'Sadko, you please me. I have thirty daughters.

You may choose the one you wish to marry.'

Sadko spoke to each daughter in turn, but none reminded him of the river by his home. Finally the youngest daughter came to talk to Sadko. She smiled so prettily at him that he quite lost his heart to her. He asked her her name, and she laughingly told him it was Volga. She showed him the bracelets and necklaces he had thrown to the river when he returned from his journeys around the world. At once he knew that this was the daughter he would marry.

When they were alone that night Sadko said to his new bride, 'My pretty Volga, your black hair shines with the brightness of stars reflected in water. Your eyes sparkle with life and are the colour of pretty fish jumping in the shallows.'

Volga smiled sadly and kissed Sadko on the cheek. 'You will remember me in your songs sometimes?' she said. 'I cannot always be with you are as we are now. Tomorrow I must turn back into a river.'

They slept holding each other tightly.

Sadko awoke feeling cold. He reached out for his wife, and his fingers touched water. He was lying on the bank of the river Volga, and the town walls of Novrogod were casting shadows across the plain in the early morning light.

SINBAD AND THE
OLD MAN OF THE SEA

ARABIAN SEA

There once was a sailor called Sinbad, who had had many adventures at sea. He had made a great fortune from the jewels and treasure he had brought back from his travels. So he settled in Baghdad, the city of peace, to enjoy a life of gracious living. But after a time he grew weary of the softness and luxury of his life. He began to hear his soul prompting him to return to the sea once more. He stood at the quayside, watching the ships being loaded with fine stuffs. He envied this merchandise that would make the journey from Baghdad to Basrah and then to the open sea beyond.

'You are a fool to tempt Destiny once more,' said Sinbad to himself, thinking of the occasions he had had lucky escapes. But his yearning to see the open sea once again left reason behind. He used all of his remaining money to buy a fine ship and hire a sturdy crew.

He sailed lightheartedly from Baghdad and their ship met favourable winds and a calm sea. After buying and selling at various ports Sinbad's ship came one day to a deserted island. They saw only one building on this island. It was a strange white dome, with no doorway or windows. Sinbad knew that this was a Rukh's egg. This was because he had once been unlucky enough to have been picked up by the talons of one of these birds. Its legs had been the size of tree trunks, and its beak like a scimitar. He never wanted to see one again!

He did not think it worth frightening the crew or passengers with his idea about the egg. Unfortunately he did not realise they would amuse themselves by throwing stones at it. The shell of the egg broke, and yellow liquid began to seep out. Everyone ran back to the ship in alarm thinking they had caused a volcano to

erupt. Sinbad ordered the ship be cast away and they sailed from the island as fast as they could.

But it was not long before two huge clouds obliterated the sun. Looking up they could see the angry parents of the Rukh egg, each holding a massive boulder in their claws. The rocks were each at least as large as the ship. Once again Destiny had written an unlucky chapter in Sinbad's story.

The first bird let loose his missile. *Whoosh!* It missed the boat by mere inches. Its impact on the water created huge waves, which tossed the boat around like a cork. The second bird let her boulder fall. It caught the stern. The ship was smashed to smithereens. Many aboard were crushed straight away, and the rest were dragged down by the waves. Sinbad alone survived. He clung on to a timber from the wrecked ship. Eventually the tide washed him ashore on another island.

He threw himself on to the beach and lay there for most of the day, exhausted and trying to regain his strength. Then he got up. What sort of island was this? Here he had been lucky. It was like a garden of Paradise. Golden fruit hung from delicate trees, cold silver streams ran through lush greenery, and humming birds flitted about with rainbow wings. There was a close carpet of scented flowers beneath his feet.

He wandered in a daze of delight amongst the beauty until night fell. But the dark had a strange

effect upon him. Although he was surrounded by tranquillity and peace, he was suddenly gripped with a cold fear. He found it impossible to sleep. When he dozed towards morning, fearful nightmares woke him again.

With the daylight came common sense. Sinbad washed away his fearful imaginings from his mind. He decided to look over the rest of the island. He walked through the gorgeous landscape until he arrived at a beautiful lake. It was surrounded by weeping trees, and was fed by a majestic waterfall.

At the far corner of the lake he could see an old man sitting, dressed in a strange outfit. It seemed to be made of leaves sewn together in some way. 'This must be a shipwrecked mariner like myself,' he thought. He made his way over to the old man to greet him.

The old man did not answer any of Sinbad's questions. Instead he signalled to him with his hands that he had a great desire to be carried over to the other side of the lake, to eat the fruit there. Sinbad thought to himself, 'If you carry this old man on your shoulders, you will be doing a good deed,' and therefore he took the old man up on to his back.

When they got to the other side of the lake, Sinbad crouched down in order that the old man could get off his shoulders. But he would not. Instead he gripped Sinbad's neck very tightly with his legs, so that he could hardly breathe. When he realised the old man had no intention of getting down from his back, Sinbad began to panic. He looked more closely at the old man's legs, and saw that they were very muscular, and covered closely with thick hair, like a buffalo hide.

Over the following weeks, the old man made Sinbad's life a misery. He never seemed to sleep, and he made Sinbad carry him all over the island as though he were a donkey. The old man was filthy in his habits and dropped his food, and worse, all over Sinbad's shoulders. Sinbad became exhausted. He doubted that he could survive much longer like this.

One day as he carried the old man around the island, he saw some large yellow gourds lying at the base of a tree, and this gave him an idea. He collected some grapes from a vine and crushed them into the empty gourd. The round dry husk was perfect for storing the crushed grapes. Then he fastened the top tightly and left it in the sun for a few days. The grapes turned to wine. He drank a little. It was just enough to ease the pain of carrying the old man on his shoulders. After a few more sips Sinbad felt a lot happier. He carried the old man as though he were a feather. He felt so happy in fact that he danced a little jig, and laughed out loud.

The old man was not at all pleased about this. He signalled jealously that Sinbad should give him the gourd. The old man drank the rest of the wine, and by the time he threw down the empty gourd he was very drunk. He mumbled to himself and lolled about on

Sinbad's shoulders. In half an hour he was fast asleep. Sinbad felt those hated legs loosening their grip from around his neck. Losing no time at all, Sinbad threw the old man off his back and left him on the ground. He lay motionless. Sinbad ran to the shore and looked in consternation for a way to leave the island.

His luck was in. A ship was moving across the horizon. If only he could make them see him on the shore. He shouted and waved his arms about, afraid that at any minute the old man would wake up and wreak some terrible revenge on him. He undid the stuff of his turban and waved it furiously in the breeze. The ship saw his distress signal, and sent a small boat to the shore to collect him.

When he was aboard the ship he told of his experiences on the island with the old man. The sailors looked at him in awe. 'It was the Old Man of the Sea that you met,' they said to him, 'and no mariner has ever escaped his clutches before.'

OLOKUN AND THE CHAMELEON

BIGHT OF BENIN

The great and powerful Olokun, God of the Sea, sat in his underwater palace. Two crocodiles were holding him up, partly because he was very fat, and partly because he was so important that it was decided his two mudfish legs could never touch the floor. Olokun wore his best outfit, with a coral necklace that was wound round and round his neck until it reached his chin. He looked around the room and tutted. He was not in a good mood. He was waiting for the yearly coral ceremony to begin.

A long time ago the Oba, or king, of the people that lived on dry land had stolen one of Olokun's magic coral necklaces. When the Oba wore it everything he said came true. Olokun let the king keep the necklace, as long as every year, his subjects brought gifts of jewels and money to Olokun's palace under the sea.

Olokun liked to be made a fuss of. When he felt the people on land loved him he would make sure their crops grew straight in the fields, and that their cattle had enough to eat. But when he felt neglected by the people he sent frogs and crocodiles into their homes to frighten them, and spread disease. The Oba's people tried to keep Olokun happy.

Today, the day of the coral ceremony, a great snaking line of people waited to cross the bridge into Olokun's world. The ordinary men walked on foot, holding bags of coins to give to the sea god. The noblemen came on horses, with their servants walking beside them. They carried little fish nets full of gifts, which they rattled with their hands as they progressed. They all passed

47

through the gates of the palace, where the crocodile policemen were ticking off their names from a list.

Olokun sat in his Great Hall with his chief crocodile on one side of him, and his pet snake winding himself around his arms. The noblemen passed Olokun one by one and emptied their fishing nets on the ground in front of him. The jewels were sorted into colour and size. At the end of the day Olokun said that he was pleased and he agreed to meet the Oba for a talk.

The Oba was carried in and he immediately began to flatter the sea god. 'Oh Great Olokun, my people are grateful to you for so many reasons. You enrich our lives in every way, making us rich and comfortable. Because of you our children are healthy, and the crops grow straight in the fields. We know that you are even more splendid than Olorun, owner of the sky. Your palace is the most magnificent in the world. You are without a doubt the greatest of the gods.'

Olokun bowed his head regally and his insides felt puffed up like the gills of the lung fish when he takes a gasp before going ashore to wriggle in the long grass.

After the retinue had left for dry land, Olokun sat thinking over what the Oba had said to him. Perhaps he should make the people choose between him and the Owner of the Sky? If the people wanted him as their god, then they could have him. He called for the chief crocodile, and asked for a challenge to be arranged that would prove once and for all which god was the greatest. The God of the Sea would challenge the Owner of the Sky to a competition. Both gods would appear in their finest costumes, and the winner would be chosen by the Oba and his people. 'Tell Olorun that he was once a great god, but now he is too remote. He has lost his place in the people's hearts. His time is over.'

The chief crocodile wrote all this down and gave it to the chief frog, who took it to the python and he took it to Olorun in the sky.

'Tell Olokun I accept his challenge,' said Olorun, who sat in the empty acres of the sky playing chess with the clever chameleon.

A great deal of activity went on in the underwater world in the following days! The busy sea spiders wove silver seaweed into shimmering wraps of cloth. The oysters gave up their lustre to decorate the outfit. The edges were bound with tiny rows of fluted shells. The cloth was covered with starfish and sea anenomes. And of course there was coral. Olokun's head-dress was magnificent. It rose up from his forehead in tentacled tiers. Long strings of coral swung about his ears. His necklace reached up to his lips in heavy swathes. Even his mudfish legs wore splendid outfits. They flapped their fins appreciatively in their embroidered caps.

Olokun was ready to meet Olorun now. As he was carried into the Great Hall by seven crocodiles the whole of his court burst into applause. They could not imagine a more majestic sight!

There was a knock at the door. 'Who is it?' asked the crocodile,

winking at Olokun, who chuckled merrily at the thought of what power would soon be his.

'It is the chameleon, messenger of Olorun, come to escort the god Olokun to the palace in the sky for the judging.'

'Let him come in,' said Olokun.

The chameleon entered the room and a gasp escaped from the lips of all present. For the chameleon was dressed in finery every bit as majestic as Olokun's own. There was the silver cloth, the oyster lustre, the little pink beads, the rows of heavy coral.

'What impertinence is this?' said Olokun. 'The god Olorun sends his messenger dressed as the God of the Sea? Tell Olorun I will not be the butt of his poor jokes.'

The chameleon left for the sky.

Olokun had bought some time to prepare an even better outfit.

The golden sand of the coast was spun into thick thread and woven into velvety cloth. Olokun's crocodiles bullied the fish in to giving up their scales for sequins. The teeth of sharks were strung together into fearsome breastplates. The edges of his new costume were bound with tiny snakes, and on his legs crouched hundreds of little green frogs, their eyes darting in fear. His head-dress was even more magnificent. Olokun's necklace was so thick and tall that he could hardly breathe underneath it. The cool coral knocked against his teeth as he spoke. His hair was full of beads and pearls. He wore his python as an armlet. He was supported by twelve crocodiles.

'Let the chameleon enter now!' said Olokun through gritted teeth.

When the creature reached the podium it was clear for all to see that his outfit easily matched the glory of Olokun's own. 'What! Again?' thought Olokun. 'My rival must be powerful if his messenger is dressed as finely as myself.'

He looked at the chameleon, and said, 'You must forgive me, but there are some final adjustments to my costume that must be made. Please could you wait outside the door.'

As soon as the door was shut Olokun hissed 'Quickly! Bring me the eyes of fishes! The tentacles of octopi! The whiskers of catfish! The paws of crocodile! I must improve my outfit!'

The creatures looked at him suspiciously. They did not like the new tone in Olokun's voice.

52

Silently the little frogs hopped off the mudfish legs. The starfish unglued themselves from the costume, and even the python unwound himself from the sturdy arm of the god. Soon Olokun was standing in his beautiful robe devoid of ornament. He knew he was beaten. 'Tell the chameleon to go back to Olorun with the news that I no longer want to challenge him. A god whose messenger wears clothes that can match my finest. He must be glorious beyond imagination. I

concede defeat without a contest.' With that he sank into his chair waving to the catfish to unravel his coral necklace before he choked on it.

The chameleon skipped out of the palace, and the crocodiles guarding the door were amazed to see him changing his colour as he passed each rock and plant. Leaving the sea for the land he looked backwards out of one eye and winked at them. Then he turned to pale blue and leapt into the sky.

MANU AND THE RED FISH

Manu the king woke up one morning and went to look for his son.

'I have decided that the kingly life is not for me,' he said. 'I am going to the forest to live in a little hut. You may run the kingdom from now on.'

Manu took off his costly robes and laid them on a chair. He did not want to have to think about politics and tax any more. He wanted to walk in the cool shady paths of the forest and watch the birds flitting about in the trees above.

Every day at the hermitage in the forest, Manu would get up and give praise to God for all the life he saw going on around him. He would give thanks for the animals that lived on the earth, those that lived in the sky and finally he would make a blessing for those that lived in the water.

As he sat meditating one day he heard a voice saying to him 'Manu, we in heaven have noticed how you love the animals, even the smallest creatures. We would like to reward you.'

Manu said, 'I thank you, and humbly ask that I may protect them from harm.'

The voice said, 'You have chosen a difficult task Manu, we shall see.'

Manu felt soft petals of the lotus blossom falling on to him and knew he had been blessed.

A few days later Manu was carefully preparing a water blessing at his hermitage. As he lifted the water from the well, he found a little red fish in his cupped hands. He put the fish into his wooden bowl. It swam around happily. 'What a pretty little fish you are!' he said. 'I would like to take you back to my hermitage and look after you.'

Overnight the fish grew to the size of a man's hand, and no longer fitted in the wooden bowl. 'Save me! Save me!' the fish cried out in a little voice. It had grown pale, and its gills were gasping in the harsh air. Quickly Manu ran with the fish and put it in his pitcher, where it sucked the water greedily and returned to its former colour.

The next day the fish was bigger again. It had grown to the size of a man's leg. 'Please save me!' it cried out, hardly able to move in the narrow pitcher.

Manu put the fish in the well. When it got too big for the well, he took it to a pond. The fish was now almost as big as a horse. Its back stuck out of the water and its scales looked dry and papery. There just was not enough water in the pond for it to survive. 'Oh save me! Save me!' the fish called out miserably.

Manu felt upset that he could not find a home for the fish that it could live in safely. He decided to take it to the river Ganges, which surely would be big

enough to hold it. He wrapped the fish in wet cloths and covered them with mud. Then he ran as fast as he could to the river with the fish in his arms, and threw it in. The next day Manu went to see how it was, and found all the river at a standstill for the fish had grown so large it was touching the bank at each side. When the fish saw Manu it rolled its eyes and said, 'Save me! Save me!'

Manu knew there was only one thing to do. He made a stretcher out of wood and put the fish on to it. He covered the fish with wet blankets, and in the heat of the day he ran to the sea and tipped the fish in. He looked anxiously into the water to see if the fish was all right. It was already swelling before his eyes. By evening it had filled the entire bay.

'What kind of fish are you?' called Manu. 'What kind of magic is in you to make you grow so quickly?'

The fish flapped some sea water around its gills and said. 'Manu, you have shown me great kindness and spent much time and effort in keeping me alive. I was sent as a test for you by God. He wanted to see whether you had the qualities to be Protector of the creatures. I am to tell you that you have been chosen.'

'My name is Matsya, and I will help you, as you have helped me. Soon there will be a great flood. The forests and mountains will disappear under the water. All the oceans of the world will join together, and there will be a single sheet of water covering the earth.

When this time comes, you will find a boat made for you in the forest clearing. In it you must put the seeds and eggs of every living creature. You must protect them from harm and take them to a new world.'

Manu was stunned by the size of the task he had been given. Questions crowded in to his mind. 'How long have I got before the flood?' he said. 'How shall I collect all the creatures? How shall I protect them?'

The fish smiled and said, 'Manu, Manu, do not worry, all will happen as it should.' Then he hauled himself to the mouth of the bay and dived into deep waters.

Manu began to collect the seeds and eggs of all the creatures. He wrapped up the seeds of plants and labelled them each with a picture. He made boxes with soft linings for the birds' eggs, and made sure they were kept warm. He put tadpoles into little bottles and stored all the eggs and seeds of the other animals in special round boxes, with the animal's picture on the lid. Each animal was carefully noted in a ledger to make sure none were left out, or put in twice.

One day, as he sat by his hermitage, checking through the catalogue of creatures, he felt a large raindrop fall on to his hand. He looked up and saw large clouds moving rapidly across the sky. He heard the rattle and hiss of rain falling on to leaves and soaking into the hot earth. Soon the paths were muddy and slippery. Manu carried the boxes to the forest clearing, and saw the boat waiting for him there.

One by one he loaded the boxes on to the boat and fastened them down. The water was rising every minute. The boat gave a lurch as it came away from the land. Rain was falling in thick columns. Manu put a tarpaulin over his head and huddled himself close to the boxes. Days passed and still the rain did not stop. Then one morning the sun rose. When Manu looked out there was only stillness.

He was in the middle of an endless sheet of water. It was as still as a pond, without a ripple. The sky was reflected in every detail as though it was a mirror. There were no mountains, no forests, no birds in the sky. Manu was grateful for the life that he kept safe on his ship.

A black cloud appeared in the sky and blew a great wind across the water. Soon after there was a crack of thunder and it began to rain again. Waves ran across the floodwater and crashed into the boat. Manu was afraid that it would be tipped over and all the boxes would be spilt into the water. He stood up and cried out into the storm, 'Shall we perish in this storm? How can I protect these creatures in my care? Please Save us! Save us!' he cried out into the wind and rain.

He began to despair for his life, when he saw Matsya the fish swimming towards the boat. The red fish called out, 'Tie a rope around my fin and I will take you to safety away from the storm.'

Manu laughed with joy, he was so relieved to see Matsya the fish, and he threw a rope over its vast fin. Soon they were far away from the storm, and in calm waters again. The fish said to Manu, 'You saved my life many times, I am pleased now to save yours. Whenever you are in danger, just call out for me and I will come.'

After forty days the water began to subside.

Mountains and bare earth began to appear. It did not look like the world Manu used to know. He took the boxes from the boat and began to plant the seeds. He built a mud hut and carefully hatched out the eggs. After a time green shoots appeared and there were birds in the sky. Manu went to the edge of the sea and looked to where it joined the sky. He could see a red line on the horizon. It might have been the back of a huge fish, or it might have been the sun appearing for the new day.

In the Palace of Tangora

Rua-te-papuke's son wanted to go out with is older brothers on a fishing trip. His father, the chief of the compound, was concerned that he should know how dangerous it was. Before he would give his permission for his son to go fishing Rua-te-papuke needed to warn his son of the dangers that could face him. So he took the boy for a walk along the cliff path until they reached a tree hanging from the cliff-face.

'My son, you may want to go out into deep waters with your brothers, but remember that there are sea spirits waiting to snatch you and take you to the palace of Tangora under the sea. If you are not careful you may never return from this trip.'

'Who is Tangora, father?' the little boy asked.

'Do you see that tree hanging there?' Rua-te-papuke said. 'It is the entrance to Tangora's world. One day your soul will leave your body and it will make its way to here. It is called Te Reinga or the Leaping Place. Once your soul has jumped in to the sea it has to make a long journey to Tangora's palace under the sea. He is the God of the Sea and is the brother of Tane, the god who looks after us on land. When we take fishes from the sea we are stealing from Tangora, and sometimes he gets angry. Do not forget that it is a dangerous thing you want to do, my boy.'

'How far is Tangora's palace, is it a long way away?' said the boy.

'It is a long way for you, for you are small. First you must go past the underwater caves that hold the bones of your ancestors. You must not speak to them, but leave a gift to show your respect. Then you pass the floating islands of Hauraki Gulf. You must not stay in their blue domain or you will forget who you have been. After a long while you will reach the Te Wai Ora Tare, or the living waters of Tane, which you must cross. It is here that you must say goodbye to your earthly existence and become a child of Tangora.'

'Is there no way back from under the sea, Father?' the child asked.

'It has sometimes been known for people to return,' his father replied. 'But if you have eaten anything while you are underwater then you must stay there for ever.' Rua-te-papuke was silent, looking out across the water.

The next day the boat was made ready and each boy was given a fishing hook according to their size. The youngest son was given a very small hook, because he was not as strong as the others. A big fish could drag him out of the boat. Then they pushed out into the water. Rua-te-papuke watched as his boys rowed off into the evening light.

That evening the boat returned without the chief's youngest boy aboard.

'What has happened?' asked Rua-te-papuke. The other boys explained that he had begged to be allowed to try a bigger hook, and in the end the second eldest had let him hold his for a while. A huge fish bit the line, and pulled the small boy overboard before anyone could catch hold of him.

All the boys were upset, and so were their mother and father. The compound was full of the sound of weeping. Rua-te-papuke decided to try and find his son. He made the brothers take him to the exact spot where the little boy had fallen from the boat. Then he dived down into the water to find him. His son was not on the sea bed. He had surely been taken to Tangora's palace.

Rua-te-papuke was the chief of the village. This gave him the power to turn into a fish. He made himself into a whale and he swam quickly to Tangora's palace.

He knew that the tides were created by Tangora's son. The water was pulled back and forth as the monster breathed in and out. He swam with the ebb tide to arrive at the palace more quickly.

Tangora's palace was a large building, low and close, constructed of bones carved as finely as spider webs. Stories were shown on the carvings. There were pictures of Tangora and his triumphs over his brother Tane. There were tall statues around the edges of the building. A large piece of wood over the door supported a number of images made from wood. Rua-te-papuke saw his son standing in the centre of this lintel. He had not yet turned to wood.

Rua-te-papuke was overjoyed to see that his son

was still alive. He took his son gently into his huge mouth. Then he swam as far as the Living Waters of Tane and left his son there. The only way the little boy could return to his family on land was to make the long journey through the sea. He must pass through the floating islands, and remember who he was. He must go past the bones of his ancestors and leave gifts of gratitude. Most importantly he must not eat a thing while he was under the sea.

Rua-te-papuke knew that his son had to make this journey alone. Sadly he swam to the shore and turned back into the chief of the island. Then he waited anxiously at Te Reinga for a sign of his youngest boy.

The small boy walked through the floating islands of Hauraki Gulf and saw glimmers of his life in the murky shadows. He saw his brothers smiling at him and telling him to come and play. He swam past the caves where his ancestors were, and heard them talking to each other. He respectfully put a conch shell in the doorway of each cave, it would listen to their conversations. He hesitated by a beautiful avenue of sea grapes. They hung down deliciously tempting him to eat them. 'Maybe just one would do no harm?' he thought to himself. As he picked the grape he dropped it on the ground. He realised he was very tired, and the sooner he finished the journey, the sooner he could rest.

Just before evening on the second day, the little boy emerged from the cave below the tree. 'May Tane be praised that you are safe,' said happy Rua-te-papuke, and wrapped a cloak around the hungry boy.

But Rua-te-papuke knew the danger was not over yet. Tangora would not let a soul leave the underworld so easily. So he ordered that a feast be prepared for that evening, and that the boy be taken to a safe place in the woods far away from the shore. Rua-te-papuke fully expected there to be guests in the village that night.

Sure enough the sea god took on human form and arrived in the evening with his courtiers, disguised as weary travellers. Rua-te-papuke and his people kept up the pretence, and a banquet was served as was the custom for strangers to the village. After an hour or two of polite conversation the sea spirits pretended to be tired and asked to be shown to their sleeping quarters for the night. Rua-te-papuke took them to a

specially prepared house, that had had all its windows and doors boarded up bar the front door. When the travellers were safely inside the door was locked and the house was set on fire. Finding no escape, the sea king and his minions were forced to change back into their spirit form. Rua-te-pauke's people stood on the beach with flaming torches as the brightly coloured spirits squeezed themselves through the cracks in the windows and flew with shrieks of rage back into the sea.

The Monk and the Water Dragon

Yellow Sea

Throughout the Far East the call had gone out for scholars to come to Qindao to unlock the golden words of a mysterious book. A merchant had brought back a beautiful casket from his travels. Inside the box were sheaves of paper closely covered with golden words. All that saw them felt sure that they said something very important.

A young monk called An-Xiu-Shi had come to Qindao from his monastery in Korea to try and read the words. He looked out of the windows from his rented room and saw the green-and-gold paint of the temple roof where the book was being safely kept.

There were pigeons roosting on the tiles and he watched them busy about their business while he wondered about the task ahead.

He leaned out of the window and looked at the passers-by below. There were children laughing and pulling dog's ears, and men carrying bundles of fish and fruit balanced on sticks held across their shoulders. A girl wandered through the hurly-burly. She was wearing a simple brown gown embroidered with red peonies, and was carrying a basket of flowers. Her long black hair was held in a pony-tail.

An-Xiu-Shi was a novice monk. He knew he should not be distracted from his prayers. But he thought this girl was beautiful. Without realising what he was doing he took the amber ring from his finger and dropped it to the ground. She looked up in surprise, then smiled at An-Xiu-Shi, and picked the ring up.

A little while later An-Xiu-Shi decided to go for a walk to the harbour to clear his mind before the big task of the golden words that afternoon. As he left the house he saw there was a single flower on the doorstep. It was a yellow chrysanthemum and its stem was wound around his own amber ring in a love knot.

An-Xiu-Shi walked along the harbour and watched the traders buying and selling aromatic spices and brightly coloured cloths from all over the world. They looked like the busy pigeons he had seen on the temple roof. He looked out to sea, and the sunlight on the water looked like a thousand chrysanthemums bursting on the surface. He thought of the girl with the brown dress and wondered if he would ever see her again.

An-Xiu-Shi made his way back to the temple. Knocking on the door he asked to be let in and to the delight of the room full of people he picked up the scroll and read the golden words. He had studied the ancient language they were written in and so could make their meaning clear to all present. An-Xiu-Shi said that the writing was called 'the Heart Sutra', that it was very old, and that it came from India. It said many things about how best to behave, to think, and how to have a happy life.

The Prefect was very pleased, he had kept the golden words safe for a long time hoping for someone to tell him what they meant. He brought his daughter to meet An-Xiu-Shi. It was the chrysanthemum girl. 'This is Flower-Song,' he said. 'She has asked to know more about the Heart Sutra.'

The monk and the girl went for long walks along the cliff-tops and talked about the meanings hidden in the Heart Sutra. They had other secrets in their hearts that they kept hidden, too shy to talk about them to each other.

'The rivers of our souls spring from the same well,' Flower-Song said shyly.

An-Xiu-Shi looked sad and said to her, 'If we are like rivers that come from the same place, we should remember where the rivers run to. Water always flows to the sea, and this is where our lives and journeys end.'

An-Xiu-Shi gave back the loveknot to Flower-Song and went back to his lodgings.

The next day he packed up his belongings and prepared to leave Qindao. He walked to the harbour and waited for the boat that would take him back to Korea. As he stood on the quay he watched the clouds scudding across the sky, blowing leaves into the water. He wished that he could stay with Flower-Song. But he knew that he must go back to his monastery where he would not be distracted from his prayers.

The junk was waiting, its single sail was an ear to the wind. He stepped aboard and the boat moved across the water. The harbour became smaller but he could still make out the people moving about carefully among the brightly coloured goods. As he watched he saw Flower-Song arrive at the edge of the quay.

She was throwing something into the water. It was a small carved casket that glinted in the sunlight. Flower-Song had put

inside it things that she felt would keep the memory of their time together safe. There was a yellow chrysanthemum, a poem, the amber ring that An-Xiu-Shi had given her, and an embroidered heart. She wanted to give the box to An-Xiu-Shi so that he would always remember her. But now she had missed him. In her frustration she threw the box into the water.

The box did not sink. It followed the wake of the junk, bobbing about on the foam. Soon it would reach the boat, and An-Xiu-Shi would pick it up out of the water. As she watched this happen Flower-Song suddenly decided that if she were to jump into the sea she would, like the box, arrive at An-Xiu-Shi's side. Without thinking she stepped off the quay.

The water was as cold and green as jade. It pressed against her face and pulled her arms away from her body. She tried to swim but found to her astonishment that she was growing. Her body was elongating in the current with every move that she made. If she pulled her shoulders forward she found she could move like a snake. She looked down at her hands and saw that they were transforming into fins. Large whiskers like a cat-fish were growing at the sides of her face. She was turning into a water dragon.

The gods had saved her from drowning because they saw how much she loved the monk An-Xiu-Shi. Flower-Song swam up to the boat just as An-Xiu-Shi was opening the box. She could see him crying as he

read the poem she had written to him. The golden ink was shining with the truth of her words.

The one I love
Is gone to the sea
What gift can I send him?
The mighty sturgeon lives in his pool
Fish have their scales to protect them
Under this sky I find no shelter for my heart.

Flower-Song was now the size of a river. She was immortal now and nothing could change her again. She gently took the ship on to her back and guided it to a safe harbour in Korea. Flower-Song was a water dragon. She could keep An-Xiu-Shi safe from harm. From now on she would protect anyone that followed their heart.

THE STORY OF SEDNA

BERING SEA

Avilayoq lived on one of the Aleutian Islands in the Bering Sea with her father. He was an old man and worried about who would protect her once he had gone. So he married her to a dog. This dog loved Avilayoq and they had five children together. But their family made so much noise that the neighbouring families asked them to leave. They went to another island, not too far away from Avilayoq's father. Every day the dog husband went to visit his father-in-law to collect some food. Because he did not have hands, only paws, the food was put into a pair of boots and hung around his neck.

One day, while her dog husband was away, Avilayoq felt a shadow over her and looked up. A large bird was hovering around, watching her with interest. That same day a strange man rowed to her island and told Avilayoq that her father was ill. She tucked her children into bed and told them to stay there until she got back. Then she got into the boat and went away with the man with a

sharp nose. He took Avilayoq far away from her father's home. Instead he brought her to his own strange island. Here he changed back into the petrel that Avilayoq had seen before. He said he would peck her eyes out if she tried to run away. The Birdman forced Avilayoq to work for him cleaning fish and looking after his home. She was very unhappy and hoped her father and husband would come looking for her.

When the dog husband returned with the boots full of food he saw his little puppy children tucked up in their beds in the middle of the day. This was not right. They should be running about on the ice. 'Where is your mother, my little pupbags?' he barked at them. They said a man had come to take her to see their grandfather. The dog went back to the old man to find out what had happened.

When Avilayoq's father realised his daughter had been tricked, he told the dog husband to return to the children and eat the food in that day's boots. Then he set out in his boat to search for Avilayoq. Along the frozen coast he looked, calling out her name, and looking into the green sea for her face. A seagull saw how

upset the old man was, and showed him the way to the Birdman's island where Avilayoq was prisoner.

Avilayoq saw her father coming towards the island and ran towards the shore. 'I'm so happy to see you Father!' she said. 'There is a frightening Birdman who is keeping me here. Let us go quickly, for he is away hunting and will be back this evening.' They pushed the boat out into the calm glassy water and started to row away from the horrible island.

The petrel, high in the sky, saw two specks moving away from his island. He swooped down to investigate. He saw that it was his precious Avilayoq who was run-ning away. He beat his wings in rage and called up a huge wind which shook the little boat.

The sea became cloudy and troubled. The girl and her father rowed faster but the storm was gathering around them, the waves were getting higher and it was hard to control the little boat. 'Oh mercy! I am an old man!' cried Avilayoq's father. 'This must be a great man whose displeasure we have aroused. I am afraid, little one. I think you should go back to him.'

Avilayoq could think of nothing worse, and shouted to her father to row faster instead. But it was no good. Her father, in his great fear, tried to push her out of the

boat saying, 'Go back to him! Go back to the Birdman!'

Avilayoq fell from the boat. She held on to the gunwale as tightly as she could, and although she could feel the waves pulling at her clothes and legs, the water dragging her down, she held on. 'Get off! Get off!' screeched her father, now demented with fear of the storm and the spirit that had created it. He took out his knife and started to chop at her hands. Still she clung on crying with pain and fear, until her fingers were all cut off. Then, with a feeling of relief, she fell into a swoon, spiralling down to the depths of the cold blue sea.

The old man rowed back to the island where the worried dog and Avilayoq's children were waiting for him. 'Have you found my wife?' the dog asked.

The old man was too ashamed to say what had happened, and instead he said, 'Come, I will take you to where she is.'

He filled the dog's boots with stones instead of food and they set out for the spot where Avilayoq had fallen from the boat. The dog sat at the helm, sentinel, impatient to see his wife again. They were rowing towards a dark patch of sea, and the dog began to twitch his nose. 'Where is my wife, old man? I want to see her.'

'Look over there, can't you see her waving to you?' The old man pointed at the empty shore. Up jumped the dog, impatiently straining to see Avilayoq. The father pushed the dog out of the boat, saying harshly, 'Go and find her at the bottom of the sea.'

All around him as he fell were gentle animals pulling him towards his new home. The joints of Avilayoq's fingers had become the animals that live in the sea. The smallest joints became seals, the larger ones became walruses, and her thumbs had become whales. To this day she lives in the gloomy underworld with her faithful dog husband. They look after the animals in the sea, and also protect fishermen.

Avilayoq's father was eaten by a polar bear not long after. Her children? They grew up into the first huskies, the dogs that the Inuit people use to this day.

THE RAVEN AND THE TIDE

NOOTKA SOUND

There was a time long ago when there was no such thing as the tide. The sea was deep everywhere. The fish lived in the shelves and gulleys down in the dark blue depths. Fishermen did not use nets or lines, but had to try and harpoon their catch by hand, swimming underwater. This was dangerous, and after a time the Elders of the village noticed that fewer and fewer men were coming back from the fishing expeditions, and so they had less and less fish to share out with the tribe.

The Elders gathered together and resolved to ask the Raven to help them. At this time in the earth's history, it was the Raven's job to put the world in order. They told him about their difficulties. The Raven said, 'I am a clever bird, and I have performed a great number of impressive tasks. But I do not know the secrets of the ocean, and I cannot make the water any shallower for your fishermen.'

The Elders sat and thought this over. Then one of them said to the Raven, 'We

sometimes see a giant far out at sea. We call him "Fog Man". He must surely know some of the ocean's secrets, perhaps you could ask him.'

The Raven flew across endless stretches of water until he saw an island, like a raft, bouncing from wave to wave. On it was seated an old old man, with grey hair flowing from under a large flat hat. The Raven shouted down to him, 'Are you Fog Man?' and in answer the giant doffed his hat. Rolls of fog billowed out from inside the rim, and soon the Raven could not see to the end of his beak. 'Stop!' he shouted, 'I have come on behalf of the Humans to ask you for help.'

The Raven explained the problem of the too-deep sea, and how the people were starving for want of food. Fog Man shrugged and said, 'I know nothing of the ocean's secrets. If it were fog that was the problem I may have been able to to do something for you.' He stared out to sea for a long time and then said, 'But, there is someone who may be able to help. I hear there is a giant who sits on the tide.'

'Where do I find him?' asked the Raven. 'And what is a tide?'

'He dwells further over to the west, and as to the tide, that is his secret.'

The Raven flew for a long time. The stretches of water were the same everywhere he went, and he soon became heartily sick of the scenery. At last he saw a mountain in the shape of a giant. He tried to land on the giant's nose, but a huge sneeze exploded from it, and blew him off course. Cautiously he flapped back over to the rocky head, and perched on the inside of the giant's huge ear. The Raven called loudly into the black tunnel next to him, 'Are you the Man who sits on the Tide?'

'Do not shout,' said the giant. 'There is no need to speak so loudly.'

'Are you the Man who sits on the Tide?' the Raven repeated. 'The Fog Man told me that you know many of the secrets of the ocean. If you are him, please could you tell me how I can make the sea shallower for the fisherman, and also, can you tell me what is a tide?'

With a voice that was thick with stone, the giant spoke rather slowly, as though he was chewing each word.

'Yes, I am the Man who sits on the Tide. I always have done this and always will. As to the secrets of the ocean, I may have known at one time how to make the sea shallower, but it is so long since I last thought about that, I have for-gotten.'

'Try and think,' said the Raven. 'It's very important.' And he told him about the poor starving fishermen and their children and wives.

'I have many secrets,' said the giant. 'But I cannot remember what they are.'

'That is only because you have nobody to tell them to. But I am here now, and you can tell me, said the Raven.'

There was a long silence.

'At least tell me what a tide is. You must know that if you are sitting on it.'

'All I know is that I have always sat on the tide, and I always will,' the giant responded.

'Then why don't you stand up, and we can see what it is,' said the Raven reasonably.

'I cannot do that!', said the giant. 'I have always sat on the ...'

'Yes, I know.' said the Raven, a little crossly.

The Raven was exasperated with the giant, and decided to find out for himself what he was sitting on. He flew away a short distance, then swooped down to where he thought the giant's posterior might be, and drove his beak in as far as it would go. 'Aaaaaaargh!' shouted the giant, and stood up holding his bottom.

The Raven was slightly taken aback with his success. And now he could hear a sound, a huge slurping, gurgling, crashing sound. He looked down at where the giant had been sitting, and saw a gaping hole in the seabed. The sound was water being pulled into the caverns of the underground world. The sea grew shallower until the Raven could see whales and fish flapping in

the shallows. 'Sit down! Sit down!' he shouted. 'Or we will lose the ocean.' There was a tremendous splash as the giant sat down, the water shot back out of the hole in a great gush. Showers of sea creatures and shells fell past the Raven.

'How did you forget a secret like that, Man who sits on the Tide? You can make the sea go up and down simply by taking your bottom off the plug-hole.'

'Oh no, I can't do that,' said the giant worriedly. 'I have always sat on the tide, and I always will. I'm not going to change the habit of a lifetime.'

'But you now have a new habit of a lifetime, which is to get up and let the water become shallower for my human fishermen. You cannot say that you have never done it, as you just have. I saw you. And you only have to do it once a day. Think of it as a routine.'

The thought took a while to circulate round the stone brain of the giant. Once it was fastened in there, it would not dislodge. 'I like routine,' said the giant. 'I have always liked routine.'

The Raven flew back to the Humans to report on what had happened. When he arrived at the village, the Elders said to him, 'What have you been doing to the sea? First there was a thick fog, and we couldn't see to the end of our noses. Then the water seemed to run away from the land, and we collected fish flapping on the shore. Then back it came, in huge crashing waves!'

'Ah,' said the Raven. 'That is because I found the Man who sits on the Tide. And now that he has learnt to stand as well as sit, he will do both every day. Soon the tides will become familiar, and part of the fisherman's knowledge.'

Some time after this, the Raven flew out once more to visit the stone giant. As he approached he saw the great mass of stone rise ponderously. The giant got to his knees, gently washed some sea water over his shoulders, and carefully sat down again. Raven called to the giant, 'What are you doing?'

The Man who sits on the Tide replied, 'I am doing what I have always done, and will always continue to do.'

NOTES

Rose Petal and the House Under the Sea   *Page 10*

The tale of the good girl who gets her reward despite the best efforts of her wicked stepmother and ugly half-sister is common all over the world. In this delightful story there is the added interesting moral that doing your housework well is vital to success, health and happiness.

Jack and the Merrow   *Page 18*

There are many sailors' superstitions associated with mermaids, Scottish selkies and merrows. They are nearly always amoral and immortal, and generally attempt to lure sailors into danger. In this story, the merrow tries to trick Jack who is fortunately quick-witted enough to avoid the fate of other more trusting sailors.

The Sea Cow   *Page 24*

Another fairly common motif in stories about the sea is that of the gift from the sea. These stories usually feature a man and his wife – and the wife invariably gets more than she bargained for when she greedily takes delivery of the gift.

Sadko *Page 30*

Stories about a person who goes to the sea king's palace are found throughout the world. Usually when they return, they find that hundreds of years have passed even though they themselves felt that they were away a relatively short time.

Sinbad and the Old Man of the Sea *Page 38*

In this story, the old man on the island, in some ways, symbolises the sea. He is a hard taskmaster as well as being cruel and brutal. Sinbad has to struggle hard against his grip to ensure his survival and eventual return to safe port. Of course, Sinbad had many more exciting adventures – most of them at sea.

Olokun and the Chameleon *Page 46*

The Benin have beautiful, very intricately patterned sculpture which has been used as reference for the illustrations in this story. This story illustrates the way in which clothing plays an important part in the Oba's power. He would have worn garments completely covered in coral as well as a crown made of coral.   Coral is believed to have magical powers and also represents prosperity. The story happily illustrates the fact that even a king can be outwitted by a clever and wily opponent.

Manu and the Red Fish   *Page 54*

This is an Indian story very similar to the Christian story of Noah's Ark. Manu, like Noah, helps save all the animals and plants of the earth by packing them up and taking them on board a boat while the flood rages. Like Noah, Manu is chosen by the gods to save earth's creatures because of his goodness and kindness. In this story Manu saves a fish who, because of his kindness, warns Manu about the flood.

In the Palace of Tangora   *Page 62*

The sea is often portrayed in stories as a dangerous and challenging place in which the unwary visitor must exercise great caution in order for them to return to their original home. Escape from the undersea world always comes with certain conditions, often that the traveller must not eat anything while there. In this delightful version of these events it is a young boy who must use his initiative and intelligence to avoid eternity in the undersea world.

The Monk and the Water Dragon   *Page 70*

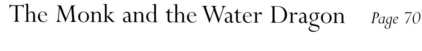

In this intriguing story, the box which Flower-Song floats out to sea represents not only a maidens love but also information and knowledge about the Buddhist faith. The sea is shown to be a vehicle and means by which Buddhism could spread around the world.

The Story of Sedna *Page 78*

This story seeks to explain how the animals and fishes of the ocean came in to existence. In Eskimo culture, the story-teller would wear a mask when telling the story, which would have all the elements of the story shown in symbolic form around the edges. Eskimo art has tremendous clarity, and is able to show the frightening and inhospitable, making it simple and compelling by dealing with it in an unsensational manner.

The Raven and the Tide *Page 84*

The raven is an important figure in American Indian mythology. It is an intermediary between the world of gods and that of men. In this story the raven acts on behalf of the humans to help people have control over the sea.

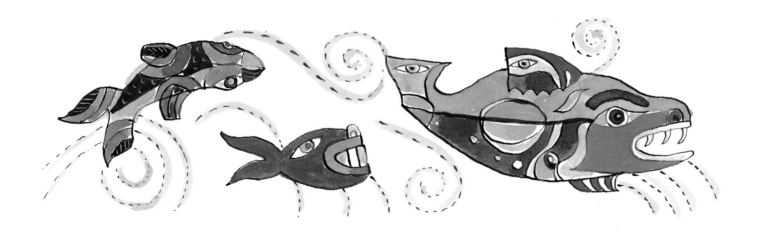